Deadly Decisions

Books By Rebecca Hemlock

Arctic Adventure series
Bitter Betrayal
Deadly Decisions

Granton House Mysteries
The Secret of the 14th Room
The Secret Diary of Deadly Deception

Copyright ©2021 Rebecca Coram
Author: Rebecca Hemlock
Design: Bluecap Publishing
All rights reserved.
No part of this book may be used or reproduced by any means, graphic, electronic, or mechanical, including photocopying, recording, taping, or by any information storage retrieval system without the written permission of the copyright holder except in the case of brief quotations embodied in critical articles and reviews.

Any reference to historical events, real people, or real places is used fictitiously. Names, characters, and places are products of the author's imagination. The views expressed in this work are solely those of the author and may not necessarily reflect the views of the publisher.

Bluecap Publishing

Ashland, KY 41102

bluecapbooks@gmail.com

bluecapbooks.com

Let all bitterness, and wrath, and anger, and clamour, and evil speaking, be put away from you, with all malice-
Ephisians 4:31 (KJV)

Deadly Decisions

Part III

Chapter 1

"Luke, are you even listening to me?" A female voice spoke. I blinked my eyes quickly, trying to collect my thoughts. My sister Stephanie sat in front of me in her favorite antique armchair. She leaned forward, staring at me with growing concern.

I quickly tried to calculate how long she was talking to figure out how much I missed. Had she changed topics?

"I'm sorry, Steph. You're gonna need to run that by me again," I admitted apologetically, rubbing my aching temple. A dull headache had settled there. I couldn't decide if it was from lack of sleep or the stressful events of the last year.

It had been 2 days since I received a phone call from my friend, Nicole, telling me that I had been betrayed by someone I was extremely close to. My dear colleague and role model, Seamore.

He'd sold me out, and I had no intention of letting him get away with it, especially after finding out that Seamore paid a suspicious visit to my sister.

"There's no sense in repeating myself. You're too exhausted to hear what I have to say," Stephanie responded. Her voice had a trace of the same defensive, hurtful tone she had when we were children when I'd done something wrong.

Times were simple back then, and I was starting to miss them now more than ever. She was right about me being exhausted though; I hadn't slept a wink since Norway.

"Why don't you go to bed, and we can talk things over later," Stephanie urged me. I felt like a child. I wasn't sure if it was because Stephanie looked so much like our mom or because she and Tom were trying for a baby and the motherly instincts kicked in early.

"I think maybe a little walk outside will clear my head," I replied. Considering the several attempts on my life, I didn't feel comfortable sleeping right now. I stood to my feet and stretched.

"Why don't you come along? Tom can keep an eye on Adam while we catch up." I offered. Stephanie looked at the doorway that led into the kitchen. Her six foot four husband was standing at the kitchen sink washing dishes. I could see that she was puzzling if Tom could spare her for a minute or not.

"C'mon, Steph. We haven't done anything together in a long time," I gently shoved her with my elbow, trying to bring the brotherly side of myself back to the surface.

"Hold your horses, Kumquat. Let me go let Tom know," She replied, holding her hands up in surrender. I watched her disappear into the kitchen. I couldn't wait to get out into the familiar woods that surrounded Tom and Stephanie's house.

I silently thanked God for the thousandth time they somehow managed to buy our grandparents' old place in Carrollton, Kentucky.

Stephanie and I spent so many summers here when we were kids. This was our safe haven after our dad died.

As I stood waiting on the front porch, I took in the view I knew so well. A tree line of tall pines stood like guards surrounding the farm with towering green mountain peaks towering behind them.

The air was sweet with the scent of honeysuckle, and a cool breeze blew so gently like a caress on the cheek. I have traveled to so many places, but none of them felt like home the way this place does.

"Are you ready?" Stephanie said, stepping out the door. She had put some hiking boots on and tied her hair up on the top of her head in a floppy brunette pom pom. I snickered.

"What?" She frowned at me in confusion, then noticed that I was laughing at how ridiculous her hair looked.

"We're going for a hike, so shut up," She then leaped off the porch and started for the trail. I quickly followed. Once I caught up to her, I could already tell that the Appalachian air was doing me good.

"So, tell me again what made you so suspicious about Seamore," I said. Stephanie looked ahead as she spoke.

"The first thing that seemed odd was when he showed up here unexpectedly and alone. Usually, you guys come here together. I tried to call you but couldn't get through, so since it was Seamore, I just let the weird feeling go. Then I caught him going through Adam's suitcase," Stephanie shrugged and looked at me.

"Then he kept asking me about the mail, like every day. Like he was expecting something. Seamore overheard Tom tell me that he would ask one of his cop friends to come out for a visit. The next thing I knew, he was gone. That same day was when Nicole called me to check on Adam and told me that you were in Norway,"

I muddled her story over. "I really feel like Seamore has stabbed me in the back," I told her.

"Luke, tell me what's really going on. Nicole said someone tried to kill you, and it freaked me out," Stephanie demanded.

I took a deep breath deciding if it was a good idea to tell her what was going on. Stephanie was one of the strongest women I knew, but more importantly, she was my sister. I didn't want to get her mixed up in this mess, but I knew if I didn't tell her, she would worry herself half to death. I decided to go ahead and tell her.

"Remember that ring I told you about?" I began trying to find the right words to soften the blow that someone tried to kill me…. again.

"Yeah, I thought that whole thing was over," She replied.

"I know I said it was. But a few weeks ago, I realized that someone was following me,"

"How do you know that?" She questioned. I was already regretting telling her this. As I explained my camping trip and the strange car speeding away, I watched her face change from concern to alarm. I could see the worry spread across her face, and I hadn't even dropped the big bomb on her yet.

"I have to leave again. Tonight," I finished, waiting for a response, expecting the worst.

"Ok, now I know you've lost it," she said, letting her open palms drop, making a slapping sound on her jeans. She walked over to a fallen tree and sat herself down on it. She stared at the ground. I could tell that she was processing everything I'd told her. I gave her a minute to think, taking the time to take in our surroundings. The birds seemed to sing sweeter here, but it was hard to enjoy it because there weren't many times that I came here on a positive note.

Several minutes passed before Stephanie spoke. I was just about to ask her to say something when she finally did speak.

"Luke, I really feel like you need to put this whole ring thing behind you and get your priorities straight. You've been trapesing all over the globe when your family needs you. Your son needs you,"

Stephanie urged. Her pleading tone tore at my soul. When she married Thomas Ross, I decided that she would be well taken care of, and that was that.

I figured I wasn't needed in her life anymore. I had to say goodbye to that big brother, protector side of myself.

"You probably think I'm crazy for this, Steph, but it's like this is calling me. Also, I've nearly been killed twice over this, and I feel that the fight isn't over. I want to protect you and Adam before things get any worse,"

The look she gave me said that she wasn't convinced that I was doing this for her sake and Adam's. I knew she probably thought I was doing this for myself. I never could resist a mystery. I had to prove to her that I was telling the truth about my intentions, but I had to admit to myself that she wasn't wrong.

"I really hate having to say this, But I want you to know that if anything happens, Adam will always have a home with Tom and me," Her words settled over me like icy rain. I didn't like hearing that for the simple fact that she felt like something was going to happen. I was glad though, that my boy would be looked after.

"Tell me where you're going," Stephanie demanded. I tossed the idea around in my mind if it was wise to tell her that.

Would it be putting my family in jeopardy? What if Seamore came back demanding to know? But if something happened and I was captured again, I would feel better if people knew where to look for me. I decided to meet myself in the middle.

"Greenland," was my reply. She seemed satisfied with that answer.

"Luke, have you considered that Seamore may be in trouble, and maybe that's the reason for his strange behavior?" She inquired. I had to admit I hadn't considered that. I was a little quick to jump to the conclusion of betrayal. Guilt started to nibble at the pit of my stomach.

"Not really," was the response I gave.

"C'mon, let's see if I'm still a better rock climber than you," Steph challenged. I welcomed the change of subject. I let myself smile even though I knew what she was doing. She wanted this to be a positive time spent together.... just in case.

Stephanie got up from the fallen tree and started briskly walking down the path toward the hills that looked to be a few miles away but were actually about a twenty minute walk.

My heart began to pound as I hurried to catch up with her. My childish sibling-competitive instances came back along with a feeling I couldn't ignore. Someone was watching us. I did a quick scan of the woods as my stomach filled with dread. Was this my life now? Will I ever feel peace or feel safe ever again?

"Hurry up, kumquat," She called over her shoulder, pulling me back to our race. I really hated that nickname. I told myself to get a grip. I couldn't lose it in front of my sister. I started jogging.

She looked surprised when I rushed past her and got about ten yards ahead of her before slowing down. She began running to try and pass me again. That was when I took off. I hadn't felt so free in a long time. I could hear her footsteps coming up behind me. She was gaining on me quicker than I had anticipated. I couldn't help but smile at the fact that I was winning.

It wasn't long before the curvy path in front of us started to grow steep. My thighs burned as my feet pushed my body uphill. Memories of my younger self running this same path flashed in my mind.

I was a few feet from the hilltop where highway 68 snaked over the peak.

Once I made it to the clearing, I saw something that brought dread back and sent it throughout my body. Parked on the side of the road was a car that looked very familiar to me. I couldn't think of any reason for it sitting there since there weren't any houses around for miles, and the car didn't appear to be broken down.

The suspicious car parked randomly on the side of the road about half a mile from my sister's house wasn't what frightened me. What scared me and concerned me was the license plate number. QH-1546. The same number was on the car that was parked near the spot where I was camping a few weeks ago.

"What's up?" Stephanie said, appearing at my side causing me to jump.

"That's a little odd. Nobody around here ever gets stuck on the hilltop. If someone breaks down up here, they usually push their car over and ride the hill down to the Sheriff's office for help," Steph explained.

'That car isn't from around here," I mumbled, looking around to see if I could spot anyone in the woods watching us. Stephanie immediately caught on that I was on high alert.

"Luke, let's go back," She tugged at my arm, pulling me back down the hill. I pulled against her.

"I'm gonna figure out once and for all whose car this is," I started looking her in the eye. Her fright worsened as the realization hit her that I'd seen the car before. I marched forward, across the narrow road and further into the woods.

"Luke, we need to get out of here! You need to think of Adam right now," Stephanie pleaded. I turned to look at her.

"I am! I won't let him spend his life in the shadow of a coward," I replied. Before I could continue, the sound of two gunshots echoed through the forest. The first bullet whizzed past mine and Stephanie's heads. The second settling in the back of my arm.

Chapter 2

Stephanie and I ran back down the way we came, ducking our heads as we heard the footsteps of the shooter coming up behind us. A few more shots fired as we leaped over bushes and thorny brush along the forest floor.

My first instinct when the first shot was fired was to hide in the woods. I figured that maybe the thick threes would serve as a shield, but since this person is chasing us, we may have stood a better chance at outrunning him.

I tried to lead my sister back to the trail, pulling her along as hard as I could. I could see the end of the path coming into view ahead.

My lungs burned, but my desire to protect my sister pushed me on.

"What are you doing?" She pulled her arm out of my grasp. It took me a few steps to stop, but when I did, I turned and reached back to grab her wrist again.

"We can outrun him on the trail," I huffed, pulling her along once again.

"Yeah and be an easier target. I'm not going out in the open," Stephanie responded.

"Steph, we don't have time to argue about this!" I urged.

"I know," she then grabbed my wrist and pulled me in the other direction. We were running along the trail home just inside the tree line, just out of sight. Part of me hoped that Stephanie's plan would work better than mine. What is one supposed to do when they are being shot at? How are they supposed to come up with a full proof plan?

I let Stephanie pull me along a route she seemed to know very well. That was when I noticed that we were moving along a bit faster than when I was in the lead.

We were about one hundred yards from the house when I saw a boulder just ahead. It was almost as big as a semi. I was just about to suggest we duck behind it to catch our breath for a few seconds when Stephanie had the exact same idea.

My chest heaved as my heart pounded. Who was this person, and why exactly were they trying to kill me? I had some idea why, but I needed more than just the fact that they were somehow connected to Lee.

I covered my mouth to try and keep as quiet as I could. Stephanie mimicked me. We heard the sound of footsteps getting closer. They slowed. Whoever was following us knew that we had stopped to hide. The forest grew quiet. I held my finger up to my sister, silently telling her to wait right there. She nodded in response.

I circled the rock, peeking around to see if I could get a sight of who was chasing us. That was when I caught sight of a dark green jacket and tan pants. It was a man with fiery red hair that seemed to be thinning on the top. I counted in my head.

3, 2, 1-

I leaped from behind the rock pushing as hard as I could on the red-haired man's back, sending him to the ground. I heard him let out a grunt as his face hit the ground.

"Who are you?!" I growled as I held him down. That was when Stephanie came out from behind the rock. The attacker silently fought to get back up. Stephanie reached for the lump in his back pocket and pulled out a black leather wallet.

"It says here that his name is Larry Hartford," She stated.

"Call the police," I grunted, pushing the rifle a few feet away. Stephanie hurried back toward the house, pulling her cell phone from her pocket. I saw her dial as she ran and placed the phone to her ear. I knew she was going to send Tom back to help me.

*****

I sat quietly at the police station, waiting for my turn to give a statement. I wanted to be relieved that we'd caught the guy, but something in the pit of my stomach told me that this wasn't over.

I had a gut feeling that someone was still following me, watching me. I went over the incident of my camping trip in my mind making sure I wouldn't forget to tell the police every detail of that night.

"You can come in now," a voice called from the doorway across the room. The Sheriff's presence told me that they had just finished interviewing Stephanie. She wouldn't know any more than what had happened to us earlier.

The large room I was led into had a table with two chairs on either side. The stone walls were painted mint green. It felt more like a bedroom or a child's playroom than an interrogation room. The Sheriff must have noticed the strange expression on my wandering face.

"Yeah, this used to be the school. This was a storage room for sports gear. There's talk of repainting, but I like this color. Plus, the color green is supposed to relax you, so it makes for better police interviews,"

The Sheriff grunted as he pulled out his chair.

He placed a small recorder on the table, then scooted the chair back a few inches to make room for his barrel chest. His big brown mustache twitched as he adjusted the settings on the small device.

"My sister and I only came to town once in a while as kids. We were here to stay with our grandparents. They never brought us to town." I rubbed my hands together as I spoke.

I had no idea why I was nervous or why I was telling him these details about myself. I was there to give a statement on the attempt on my life. The Sheriff noticed my fidgeting.

"It's alright. Once I hit the record button, I'm going to ask you questions and we'll just have a regular conversation," he said soothingly. His soft tone made me feel a little bit better. He pressed down on the button and began to speak.

"My name is Sheriff Brady..." He began. I listen to him state all the information needed for documentation. It did not feel like a regular conversation so far.

"Tell me what happened this morning Luke," Brady finally asked.

I went through the event, telling him step by step about my conversation with Stephanie about our walk.

"Did you see Mr. Hartford anywhere nearby before the attack?" Brady asked me.

"No, look, this is not the way it seems. This is not the first time this guy, Hartford has come after me," Just as I was about to continue my explanation, Sheriff Brady stopped me.

"Hold on. Not the first time? I think you need to back up and tell me the whole story,"

I told him the short version of my history with Lee and about the incidents in Nunavut and in Norway.

"So an Inuit Chief helped you escape?" Brady asked halfway into my story.

"Yes, He's a great friend of mine. He's turning things around up there," I quickly answered.

I went on to tell him about the ring and how there's already been one death and one disappearance because of the ring.

"Have you already filed charges against him?" Brady interrupted again.

"Well, no. I really don't have anything to prove what he's done," I replied.

"So what you're trying to say is that Hartford was hired by Lee to kill you," Sheriff Brady deduced. I nodded. Brady pressed the button on the device to stop recording. He crossed his arms over his barrel chest.

"This is turning out to be a lot more complicated than I thought," He sighed. We sat in silence for a moment. The Policeman seemed to be in thought. I could almost see the wheels turning in his head. I really hoped he wasn't just playing along with my story. I kept telling myself that he thought I was totally crazy.

"I'll need you to stay in town for a few days until I can make some calls," He finally said. I started to protest.

"I need to get back to work. My crew-"

"Will also need to come in for questioning," Brady finished for me. Great, what had I gotten myself into. I really wished I would've kept my mouth shut about the whole thing and just told him the basics.

Brady stood and grabbed the papers and recorder. I stood and started for the door.

"Mr. Wilkins, I'm going to get to the bottom of this," He stated. I couldn't tell if he said that to make me feel better or if he suspected me of something. I was afraid of what was going through his head. I left without responding to him.

Sheriff Brady looked just like the type of person I used to wish would marry my mom. I remembered desperately wanting someone that would fill that role. It would've been nice to have someone bail me out of the messes I'd gotten myself into as a boy. Now I'm in a bigger mess and being bailed out was the least of my problems.

Chapter 3

The trip back to Stephanie's house began in silence. I stole a glance at my sister just in time to see a tear run down her cheek. She stared down the road with a look on her face that was all too familiar. I remembered seeing it on my mother's face. It was the look of sincere worry.

"Steph," I began.

"No! We were almost killed and you're gonna tell me that you're still leaving," She burst out.

"I have to," was the only thing I knew to respond with. I knew Stephanie would have a hard time with this but had no idea an attempt would be made on her life too. I had to put an end to this. Even if it meant me sacrificing myself for my family.

"You're not thinking of anybody but yourself," She continued.

"I'm only thinking of everybody else," I shot back. Stephanie pressed her lips together as if forcing herself not to say anything else.

"The more I run away from this, the more people I'm close to getting hurt. I have to put a stop to this," Stephanie kept quiet for several minutes. I hated when she did that but understood it. When we were younger, she would set her feelings aside and think about the issue in every aspect he could.

Stephanie took a sharp turn into her driveway. The steep hill curved left and right before then straightened at the bottom of the hill where the house sat. As we each climbed out of the car, Stephanie looked at me soberly. I could tell she was about to say something when I heard my favorite word.

"Dad!" Said a voice from behind me. I turned to see Adam jumping off the porch step just like Stephanie had this morning. I hadn't realized he'd picked up that habit. A quick memory of myself doing the same thing at his age flashed through my mind.

"Hey buddy," I called back. I glanced at Stephanie to see that her expression changed to a happy one.

"Uncle Tom and I have already had dinner. We had Cheeseburgers. We left some for you," Adam explained.

"Thanks," I responded.

"Uncle Tom's cheeseburgers are a little bit better than yours, Dad. He doesn't put tomatoes or lettuce on his. He puts bacon on them instead," Stephanie let out a chuckle at Adams' brutal honesty.

About an hour later, Adam went to bed. Stephanie, Tom and I began talking about the events of the day and I told them about the Sheriff's suspicious remarks toward me.

"He must think I'm somehow involved with something illegal." I finished.

"You know it was kind of stupid to tell him everything that's been going on," Stephanie pointed out.

"I know. I know. I've been telling myself that evening,"

"Luke Sherriff Brady really isn't as bad as he seems. I've known him for years and trust him completely," Tom reassured as he came into the room with two steamy cups of coffee in one hand and one in the other. I wanted to believe him, but something tugged at my insides, telling me to remain suspicious.

"I'm just curious as to what calls he could make that would help me," I replied.

"I don't know, but I would still trust him if I were you," Tom handed me the warm cup and I took a sip. The warmth going down my throat almost instantly made me drowsy.

"Well this can't wait. I need to get to Greenland and figure this out before Lee does. There's a lot about this Lachlan character that Lee doesn't know and I'm going to use that to my advantage. Plus, I don't want anyone else getting hurt," I finished ginning a pointed look toward Stephanie. Tom settled himself by Stephanie just across from me. If she was right about Seamore, he was running out of time.

"I don't fully understand why that man was sent here, nor am I happy about the fact that Stephanie was out there with you today, but I do have access to some money through my company. I can get you as far as Montreal." Tom informed me.

"That's great. Yes, thanks. I can call in some favors and figure out the rest of the trip,"
I also wanted to figure out what to say to show my appreciation for his help, but before I could Tom stood to his feet.

"Well, I'm off to get some shuteye. We've got lots of planning to do tomorrow," Tom said.

"Yeah, I'd better get some rest too before my trip. I'd like to leave as soon as possible," I added. I glanced at Stephanie to see a hint of relief on her face that I was finally gonna try to sleep.

It felt good to know that someone still worried about me. My good feeling was quickly overpowered by guilt that the events of today could've been avoided if I'd just taken her advice and rested this morning.

*****

Tom came through for me quicker than I'd expected. The following morning, he told me that he had me booked on a flight to Quebec at midnight. I was glad for the almost perfect timing.

It took most of the day but before 5pm, I had a clever disguise put together and my bags packed. It had been a while since I'd taken a trip like this by myself.

It took a few phone calls, but I'd found a connecting flight to Copenhagen from Montreal. I hated flying. I was getting to the point of never wanting to fly again, but I was here now, and I would need to fly to get back to my family.

I was really proud of my disguise. I looked much older and practiced walking with a limp to go along with the cover story I came up with about an injury on a fishing boat.

Just before I'd prepared to leave, there was a knock at the door. I opened the door to find a man in jeans, a flannel shirt, and a thick blue coat who looked a lot like Sheriff Brady from Carrollton.

"What are you doing here?" I asked, completely dumbfounded by his presence. He pushed past me into my hotel room and seated himself on the bed.

"I think we should have a little chat before you do something stupid and get yourself killed," He began pointing to the chair across from him. I knew time was growing short, and Lee would be leaving town soon. Reluctantly I sat down.

"Again, what are you doing here? How did you find me?" I questioned.

"Your sister told me where you were heading. She filled in some of the blanks for me which made your story a little more believable," He replied. I rolled my eyes. I specifically asked Stephanie not to tell anyone where I was going or why I left. Brady seemed to read my mind.

"Don't be too hard on her. She's just looking out for you,"

"Yes, well this is a very dangerous situation, and I don't think you'll be able to keep up. No offense," A pang of guilt hit me after the intentional insult.

Why I opted for the hurt-their-feelings-and-make-them-go away-angry-to-protect-them method, I'll never know. Brady didn't look that out of shape and his hands were thick with strength. I had to admit that I actually felt a little better than he was there.

"I can handle myself just fine. Maybe if we work together, we can get to the bottom of this whole thing," Brady rubbed his hands together as if anxious to get started.

"Why do you want to help me? I'm a total stranger," my distrust was still at the front of my mind and I was never one to beat around the bush. Brady stared at me for a moment. I could almost see the wheels turning in his head, debating with himself on whether he should tell me his real reason for being here for following me.

"Luke, I've wanted to make myself known to you and your sister for a long time, but the right time never seemed to come until now," Brady paused for a moment. I wanted to ask him what he meant by that but thought it best to remain silent. He chewed on his bottom lip and exhaled in such a way that made his mustache twitch.

"I knew your mother. She was a dear friend of mine right up until she died. She asked me to look after you and Stephanie, but you and Stephanie didn't really seem to need me. She got married and you started working with your dad's friend," Brady paused.

I assumed he was waiting for a response or a reaction from me. I wasn't sure what he expected from me, but the only thing I felt was anger.

"So you didn't keep your promise to her," was my response. It honestly wasn't too surprising to find out that Brady couldn't be trusted. Not in the way I'd first thought, though, so I had to give him that. He could be of help on this expedition but that was it.

I regretted the thoughts I had about him being what I wished I had in a father figure. A guy that I wished my mom would've gotten with.

"Did you love her?" I asked, trying to hold back the wave of anger and emotions that was threatening to burst out of me. I needed someone like him very much and my mom knew that.

"Yes," he replied.

"You know many times growing up, I wished I had someone I could go to for my problems. My mom wanted you to be that person. Poor choice on her part, I guess,"

I could see how much my remark stung Brady's face.

"I almost reached out to you when your wife died, Luke. I should have," Brady said apologetically.

"Stephanie has been the only mother figure he's had," I had to admit to myself that Nicole had been there for him for the last few years, but he didn't need to know that.

"I'm sorry," Brady whispered. I stood to my feet and started for the door.

"I lost my father at a young age. I really needed someone like you around. At least you being here will ensure that my son doesn't have to go through the same thing I went through," I turned the knob and pulled the door open, almost causing it to slam into the wall. Brady jumped to his feet.

"Luke. We really need to talk about this more later. Right now, you need to tell me what's going on and why we are here," Brady urged. I wanted to take a few moments to myself to think about everything he'd told me.

How he let me fend for myself as a young adult, but I knew he was right. I closed the door and sat back down. I then told him about what I suspected was Lee's plan. About the Viking Lachlan.

Brady listened intently, asking the occasional question. I wanted to hold on to the bitterness but let it go for now. I needed to trust him to have my back and I needed to have his too. It would be our best chance of survival.

Chapter 4

Brady was a huge help with planning my next move in getting the ring back from Lee. It was decided that I would look into some historical records to get an idea of where they were going while Brady tried to get us a flight to Nuuk, Greenland. I met him about two hours after our "heart to heart" at the airport.

"We were lucky to find a flight to Greenland so quickly. The lady I spoke with told me that they only charter flights once every few weeks," Brady explained, pointing to the brightly colored pamphlet he'd been given. I could tell by his excitement that he hadn't done a lot of international travel. I groaned inwardly.

Brady tried his best the entire 7 hour flight to get me to talk about myself. I tried to be cordial about it and let him know that I wasn't interested in talking. However, that didn't stop him.

He told me all about his life as a police officer and all the places he worked since leaving high school. I had to admit I was interested in the parts of his stories that were about my mom.

I could feel the temperature drop as we went further North. I stood and walked towards the back of the plane to use the lavatory when I spotted him. A man that looked a lot like Gustav "the finder" was sitting at the very back clutching a barfing bag. I thought it a little odd that a man whose job was to travel the world searching for lost objects got airsick.

I discovered that the lavatory was occupied once I got there and was forced to stand next to Gustav's seat. This was an unexpected opportunity. I pulled a peppermint out of my pocket and held it in front of him.

"These help me with air sickness," I said with a slight growl to my voice, hoping the disguise would fool him.

"Thank you," he said, taking the piece of candy from my hand and popping it into his mouth.

"Flying always does this to me," he said.

"I know what you mean," I responded.

"My name is...John," I said, struggling to find a name that would sound believable.

"Gustav," He responded. I was surprised that he used the same name as before. Maybe he didn't care so much about hiding his identity. I fought for something else to say to keep talking to him.

"What's waiting for you in Nuuk?" I asked, hoping that asking him outright wouldn't alarm him or raise suspicion.

"Business. You?"

"I am a prospector, and I hear there's gold to be had," I prayed that I wouldn't regret saying that. Gustav gave me a look that instantly sent a rush of anxiety through my body.

"You don't know how right you are. Come. Sit," he said, hoping to the next chair over leaving the aisle seat for me.

I glanced up to the front of the plane to see Brady peering over the chairs at me. Reading the look on my face he nodded that he understood why I sat with a total stranger.

Gustav told me about the Vikings and their search for new lands.

"Erik the Red prepared an expedition to the new world, which is now America, but a terrible storm came that blew them off course. Erik had 25 ships leave with him but only 14 made it to Greenland where Erik decided to settle. This is what history tells us but no one knows what happened to those 11 ships………...except me," Gustav explained.

My eyes widened. How could he know what happened to the other ships? I thought back to all the research that was left in those caves back in Norway. If he had that information, why would he leave it behind?

He continued telling me about Viking history and a few Viking battles, up until we landed in Nuuk. Before he had the chance to leave I decided to chance it and ask.

"What do you know about Lachlan?" I asked. He froze and stared at me for a moment.

"Come with me. I would like for you to have dinner with me and my friend. You don't have any appointments right away, do you?" He asked.

"Just one but it shouldn't take too long. I'd be glad to meet up with you and your friend," I responded.

"Great, meet me here then," He stood and began to write something on a piece of paper he pulled from his pocket. He handed it to me and quickly marched out of the now empty plane. I hurried off after him.

I had to find Brady and quickly make a plan. Bumping into Gustav on the plane was completely unexpected. I mumbled as I walked, trying to remember the disguised voice I used so I didn't make a mistake and use a different one later.

*****

It was decided. I would meet up with Gustav on my own with Brady always watching close by just in case anything went wrong.

I didn't know it until we went over the plan, but Brady used his law enforcement credentials to bring weapons with him. I felt a lot better about the situation that I would have a gun on my person during my meeting with Gustav.

I met with Gustav at 9pm that evening. It took me a little while to find the hotel where he was staying despite only being a few. As I walked down the chilly streets, I kept getting distracted by the beauty of the Northern hemisphere.

I wished I could remain outside to catch a glimpse of the Aurora Borealis dancing across the night sky, but I had to remember why I was here. I had to remember my mission.

I took a quick glance over my shoulder to see Brady walking about 25 yards behind me.

"We shouldn't be seen together here," He told me. I agreed.

The time on my watch read 9:02pm when I set foot in Gustav's room.

"You are late," He mumbled as he pulled me into the room and stuck his head out the door. He took a quick look in both directions and shut the door. I knew Brady would sneak to the door and listen as soon as he felt it was safe.

I didn't know if Lee or Isaac was close by or not so I told Brady not to let himself be seen by anyone. I wished I had some pictures of them to show him so he knew what to look for, but for now, we had to take this one step at a time with what he had.

"Why did you want to meet with me this evening?" I asked, hoping I had nailed the exact accent and voice tone I used earlier on the plane. Gustav didn't seem to notice any difference.

"I wanted to make you an offer of the highest secrecy," He began. He had a look of excitement on his face. I had no idea what to expect.

"I have a team that will be leaving tomorrow morning on an expedition of great historical value. I can't tell you all the details right now but it has to do with what we discussed on the plane. Are you interested?" I hesitated so that I didn't look too eager.

"Why do you need me? What would I be doing on the trip?" I asked.

"I need an assistant to help carry all of my research and help me pinpoint the location of a historical site, and your knowledge of Viking history is impressive," Gustav replied. I waited a moment to answer, looking as if I was muddling it over in my mind. This was turning out to be a lot easier than I thought it would be.

"I'll have to get some gear together quickly to be ready by the morning," I responded.

"No need. Just meet me back here, and I'll have everything you need." Gustav stuck his hand out for me to shake it. He gave me a nod of confirmation as he shook my hand with a tight grip. That was when I noticed a look in his eye. One that I did not trust one bit.

After I left, I had Brady walk with me back to the room we'd rented. I spent the entire time telling how the meeting went and the look I caught a glimpse of. Something didn't feel right. We would have to take turns sleeping tonight, just like Josh and I had done in Oslo.

The following day, I met Gustav back at his hotel. As he drove me to the outskirts of town, I peeked in the rearview mirror once to make sure I could see Brady.

"There you are, John. I'll introduce you to my associates then we will be on our way. I'd say we'll have to hike to get to the right spot." Gustav explained.

"You still haven't told me where we are going or what we are looking for," I pointed out. Gustav remained silent for a moment. I could see he was deciding how much he wanted to tell me about this. That feeling that something wasn't right returned. I always trusted that feeling. My mom used to say that it was my God-given talent. God, He and I were strangers, but he was someone I really wish I had a better relationship with.

If you're there, please keep me safe as this unfolds. I mentally prayed.

Chapter 5

When we reached the end of town, a vast white world opened up before us. Several pickup trucks and SUVs were waiting for us. As the truck came to a stop, I climbed out and met Gustav on the other side, where I found him already talking to Isaac and Lee. It was all I could do to stand there while Gustav introduced me as his assistant for the expedition.

"Good to have you aboard," Isaac said, sticking out his hand. I shook it and turned to shake Lee's hand as well. He looked me in the eye. I stared back, hoping he didn't see right through my disguise. I had a big bushy beard that looked pretty real, but I knew Lee wasn't an easy one to fool.

I let my hand drop to my side. Lee scoffed at me, then turned and made his way back to one of the trucks. He climbed up in the bed of the truck.

"Listen up!" Lee called as about a dozen men gathered around the truck bed.

"We have about an 8 hour drive then a 4-hour hike ahead of us. Those who see this through will be paid the full amount promised. Anyone who starts asking questions about the purpose of the expedition or anything else will go home empty handed," Lee glanced down where I stood as he spoke. I thought it was odd that Gustav never mentioned any sort of payment for me being his assistant. Still, I'd apparently just missed my chance to ask about it now. I would simply have to wait and ask Gustav about where we were going and why.

"Let's go!" Lee said, climbing back down from the truck. His words send everyone running to different vehicles. Before long, a caravan of cars started up a hillside highway heading North.

Both Isaac and Lee climbed into the truck with Gustav and me. The trip was one I will never forget.

The icy mountains looked similar to the ones in Nunavut, yet they were completely different. The majesty of the mighty hills took my breath away and forced me to fight back the tears.

I noticed Isaac and Gustav were talking with Lee. I couldn't make out what they were saying. Occasionally Lee would look over his shoulder at me. Worry hit my stomach. Were they on to me? I really hoped Brady was close behind. I told him to always keep us in sight just in case I needed help.

It was around 2:30 when the caravan stopped on the side of the road. Everyone jumped out and started grabbing the gear and lining up next to the cars. I hurried as quickly as I could to grab Gustav's bags. I had to make sure I looked like his assistant. I felt Lee's eyes on me and tried to listen to what he was saying to Gustav.

"We are running behind. He's not going to be happy," Lee said to Gustav in a hushed tone.

"We just need to get to the top of this ridge so I can get a better sense of direction. You can let him know we'll be back on track very soon," Gustav muttered back.

I frowned. Who were they talking about? Before I had time to figure out the answer, Gustav was at my side.

"You asked me about Lachlan when we were on the plane," He began. I met his gaze, waiting for him to finally tell me the big secret. I wondered if Lee told him to tell me or if it was Gustav's decision.

"Those 11 ships that disappeared from Erik the Red's voyage for new land were actually led by Lachlan, who tricked Erik the Red, his older brother, into showing him the way to the new land. They weren't lost in a storm but snuck away to make it to the new land first.

Lachlan wanted to form a colony of his own. When we get to the top of this hill, we are looking for any formations in the next valley that looks like it may have had a village there at some point," Gustav explained.

"So we are looking for a village site. How will we know where to look?" I asked, hiding my excitement. Lee was trying to find Lachlan's treasure using the spider ring.

"Using this," Gustav replied, pulling a piece of dark brown animal skin from his bag.

"This is written in Lachlan's own hand. He journaled many of his travels, and this part will tell us………...where to find his treasure," Gustav finished. There was no way for me to hide my shock at where Gustav held in his hand. I wanted to ask questions to make it sound like I didn't know anything about Lachlan's keep or his treasure, but I couldn't find words.

Before I had time to fully process that Gustav had part of Lachlan's journal, we were standing on top of the ridge looking out over the valley on the other side. The wind whipped hard, creating a light white haze over our view. Some of the men were having a hard time keeping their footing. I debated whether I should act the same way or not. After all, I was on this trip because of what I knew, not where I'd been.

"Do you see anything promising?" Gustav asked, appearing at my side. I scanned the valley ahead.

Then spotted something that looked like a perfect circle in the snow that looked to be just at the foot of the hill.

I took into account the perspective at a high altitude and figured it was about 2 miles away. From where we stood, it looked to be about the size of a quarter. I did the calculations in my head and decided that it had to be about half a mile in circumference. I pointed at it.

"I'd say that looks promising," I replied, returning the look of satisfaction and excitement that Gustav was giving me.

It took us what seemed like days to get down the mountainside, but after looking at my watch, only three hours had passed. As we approached it, the snow-covered bubbled towered over me about as high as a four-story building.

"Beautiful, Isn't it? But we aren't here for that," Gustav said, pulling my arm in another direction.

"What are we here for then?" I asked. As I turned, I saw a sight that sent rage and panic throughout my body.

Lee was standing about 50 yards behind me. On the ground in front of him lay Brady's motionless body. I prayed he wasn't dead.

"Luke Wilkins. You really think you had us fooled?" Lee asked rhetorically. My shoulders dropped.

"Let him go. He has nothing to do with this," I demanded.

"You're right, but he's been following us since Nuuk, so I assumed he was your lookout," Lee chuckled.

"Lachlan's gold is mine," Lee said, placing his foot on Brady's back. I charged at him. Gustav grabbed the back of my coat and shoved a pistol into my ribs.

"That's not a good idea," he said. I felt like such a fool. I told myself not to let my guard down, but that's exactly what I did.

"So this was all a big trick," I said, looking over my shoulder at Gustav.

"I'm sorry. I have no choice in this matter," He muttered in my ear. His response confused me.

"What do you mean?" I asked.

"My wife and daughter were taken. If I don't help them find this gold, I'll never see them again," I felt my anger toward Gustav soften into compassion. I knew that feeling of helplessness.

"How did you know it was me?" I asked him. Gustav's demeanor and tone changed from confident to one of a prisoner who was just following orders.

"From the moment you asked me about Lachlan. Lee told me you would show up asking questions. I instantly recognized you," I nodded. I thought I'd come up with the perfect disguise. I never figured in a million years I'd be so easily found out.

"Now, according to the journal, Lachlan did not want his gold buried inside the village because he didn't trust anyone, not even his older brother, Erik the Red," Lee began. He slowly opened the scroll and looked it over for a moment, his foot still on Brady's back. I knew I had to do something. I had to figure out a way out of here.

If Brady's injuries were worse than they looked, I would have to carry him out of here.

I wouldn't make it out alive. I would have to wait till he came to. At least Lee planned to keep me alive….for now.

Chapter 6

As Lee started in one direction, I looked off in another, hoping to stumble across some sign of life out here. I could feel the temperature dropping as evening set in. I knew from taking a peek in the back of the truck Gustav drove that there was camping equipment, so I assumed someone in the group would be setting up camp soon.

One of the men had tied Brady up and left him face down on the ground, with another man holding a 45 pistol pointing at his back. Brady strained to look up. His face was worn and weak from the blood loss. Gustav tapped my back with the 45 he held, urging me to keep walking.

The group walked for about 10 minutes before coming upon a large rock covered with snow. Lee ran his hand across it, revealing several carvings that were definitely Nordic.

"This is it," I heard Lee say. My heart sank. Lee was about to get his hands on one of the greatest treasures known to man.

"Well, Luke. It looks like I beat you to it," Lee said, turning from the massive rock to face me.

"You come from a wealthy family. What could you possibly use the treasure for?" I burst out. There was no hiding my rage at this point. I'd been rivals with him for far too long and I was ready to go head-to-head with him. I was about to charge at him again when I heard an all too familiar voice behind me.

"He's going to use it to help me finally retire," I turned to see Seamore standing next to a snowmobile.

"You" was the only word that escaped my mouth. I couldn't recall a moment in my life that I ever felt so betrayed.

"I'm amazed that you didn't figure it out sooner. All these years, you hated him because he always seemed to figure out what you were hunting for and get to the sites first. You never once suspected a mole," Seamore chuckled.

"You were like a father to me," I yelled through gritted teeth.

"I'd worked with your father for decades. He left everything we built, everything I built, to a boy who had no idea what he was doing," Seamore yelled back, taking a step toward me. I shook my head.

"I had to spend the last several years working for...you!" He said, pointing a long bony finger at me.

"Now I'll get the retirement I deserve, and Lee will take over the Alaskan Environmental Research team," Seamore finished. I didn't respond.

Seamore walked over to where Lee was standing next to the rock and held out his hand. Lee placed Lachlan's ring and his journal into Seamore's hands. Seamore looked at the artifacts for a moment. I wondered what was going through his mind.

Did he think that he'd finally gotten what he deserved, or was there a much darker plan for the riches that would be unearthed today?

Seamore slipped the ring on his finger and took 10 paces from the large stone with the Viking carvings. He knelt down and scooped the snow away until he found solid ground. As he placed the ringed hand to the ground, we heard a low rumble. The earth began to quiver. I looked at Lee then to Gustav, whose eyes were as large as saucers.

"This is the spot!" Seamore bellowed. About six men gathered around him with shovels, including Lee. They shoveled away all the snow around Seamore until he was sitting in a six foot circle.

When the large brown circle was completed, Seamore began rubbing his open hand flat on the ground again, like he was petting the dirt. The ground shook once again. What looked like molehills started forming around Seamore.

He crawled over to the nearest one and wiped the dirt away with his hands, revealing a large golden vase with strange markings on it. Seamore held the vase up in the air above his head.

"We did it!" He called out. I was dumbstruck by what I'd just witnessed. I knew there had to be some logical explanation behind it but wasn't sure how to explain it. Gustav must have seen my confusion. He took a step closer to me.

"You're having trouble figuring out how this is done," Gustav guessed. I nodded.

"Lachlan's 'magic' was just science at work. The ruby is larger than normal mixed with iron; therefore, it must have a higher magnetic pull than the average pure ruby," Gustav explained.

"Gold is not magnetic, so scientifically, this shouldn't have worked," I replied, pointing to where Seamore was still crawling on the ground.

"Gold can become magnetic if exposed to heat. Just the right amount of heat, mind you. Lachlan and Erik the Red came from Iceland to find land. Land during that time meant wealth. They must've come from Southern Iceland. I bet this gold came from the region near the volcano," Gustav started rubbing his chin as I watched the pieces fall together in his mind.

"I'm still not following you," I responded.

"The volcano must have heated the gold to a high enough temperature to make it extremely magnetic. When Lachlan discovered this, he used it to his advantage to make his followers think he possessed magic,"

"And that's how his fame grew," I finished. Erik the Red led the expedition to the new world, but Lachlan wanted the attention for himself. The bad blood between these brothers made me think about Seamore's feelings toward my father and me. Before I could even think about patching things up with Seamore, I had to get Brady and get out of here.

I glanced over to the snowmobile that Seamore appeared on. I could see from where I stood that he'd left the keys on them. Gustav looked to be about Brady's age, so I figured a blow to the gut would take him out long enough for me to make my escape. I counted in my head.

5-4-3-2-

Before I could say one, I heard the sound of a gunshot burst right in front of me. It was so loud and so close that I wondered for a second if Gustav had pulled the trigger into my ribs.

I squeezed my eyes shut but felt no pain. I opened my eyes again to see Lee pointing his pistol at Seamore, who was lying face down on the dirt.

Chapter 7

My heart broke where I stood. I couldn't move or process what just happened. Despite the betrayal, Seamore was like a father to me.

"There, that's done. He really thought we were going to share the gold with him," Lee quipped. Lee then got down where Seamore's lifeless body lay and began rubbing the dirt just like Seamore was doing just seconds before.

The second Lee turned his head to the ground, I sent a fist into Gustav's stomach.

"Sorry about this," I muttered as he doubled over in pain.

I ran as quickly as I could over to the snowmobile and ducked my head down as I sped away. Gunshots rang over my head, sending bullets whizzing by.

Thank you. I said out loud, glancing up at the sky. I had no idea how I would've escaped if Seamore hadn't driven up in the snowmobile. As we got closer to where the Viking village site was, I squinted my eyes to try and spot Brady and those guards. They were nowhere to be found. I slowed the vehicle to a stop.

"Brady?" I called out.

"Here!" I heard someone call from a rock formation about 200 yards from where I was. I drove over to where he stood, waving his arms widely.

"What in the world happened?! I was worried sick. Where are the guards?" Brady smirked at my questions.

"I told you I could handle myself. Are you alright?" He asked in return.

"Yes, but this isn't going to make it all the way back to town. We're stuck out here and have no way of getting help,"

"Well, the guy that rode that here actually came from the opposite direction that we came from," Brady informed me.

"Really? I thought there was nothing but a frozen wasteland," I questioned.

"One of the guards said the same thing, but the guy explained that there was an Inuit village in that direction," Brady replied, hopping onto the back of the snowmobile. I hoped because I was on this vehicle that whoever lived in the village didn't think I was working with Seamore and Lee.

"I can make some calls and have help here in about 12 hours," Brady told me.

"What help?" I asked. Who could this small town cop possibly know that could get help here in 12 hours? I asked myself.

This should be good. I thought as we sped off.

The village was a little farther away than I'd expected. It took us nearly 45 minutes until we first caught sight of houses.

They were painted bright colors just like the ones we had seen in Nuuk. I pulled the snowmobile near a red house and climbed off.

I had no idea who was in charge in this village or if there were police.

Brady and I made our way down the snowy street, looking for any sign of life. Someone to ask where to find the police.

"I just need to find a phone," Brady stated, huffing as he trotted past me. He climbed the porch steps of a bright blue house and knocked on the door.

"I'll check in here for a phone," He offered. I waited by the snowmobile. As the door opened, Brady was met by an older man that towered over him. Brady explained that he needed to use a phone. The middle aged man invited him in. I took a deep breath of the frigid air. I was tired of running for my life. I usually loved to travel and see the farthest corners of the world, but now I wished more than anything that I was home with my family. I missed them so much.

"Luke?" I heard a familiar voice say behind me. I turned around to see the Chief from Nunavut. He engulfed me in a hug.

"It's great to see you," he said, with a firm slap on my back.

"What on earth are you doing here?" I asked, equally glad to see him. If anyone could explain what was going on, it was him.

"I am here visiting some friends, and you?" He responded. I began explaining that I came here to chase down Lee and the ring. I gave him the quickest version possible of my trip to Norway and my entrapment in the cave there.

"All this has to do with a Viking named Lachlan who came here to settle Greenland with his brother Erik the Red," I finished.

"Do you remember the story I told you about the Viking King who Invaded and enslaved my ancestors?" He said, me recalling as he spoke. I nodded.

"That Viking king's name was Lachlan," he told me. All the pieces of the story began falling into place in my mind. They must've left Iceland on good terms. I wondered what happened between them to cause them to part ways.

That was when the Chief placed his hand on my shoulder and pulled me closer to him, then continued to speak in hushed tones.

"Not many people in my hometown know that part of the story," He continued.

"That must have been what happened to the 11 ships that disappeared in the storm when Erik the Red was on his way to Greenland," I added.

"Yes, Lachlan gained the loyalty of those ships and persuaded them to follow him. It's an interesting story," The Chief finished as Brady came out the door of the little house.

"Luke, we should have helped here in about 12 hours. We just need to lay low until then," Brady stated.

"You both can come and stay with me and my family," The Chief offered.

"That would be perfect," Brady responded. I felt awkward but reluctantly introduced Brady to the Chief, then briefly explained to each man where I'd met the other.

I still wasn't comfortable with Brady's manner. He never met a stranger, and that would get him killed if he was in this business. Thank goodness he wasn't.

The Chief led us to the house of his niece, which was about half a mile from where Brady placed his call. I was surprised just how many people lived in the village. From a distance, it looked like a few tiny houses and one or two bigger buildings.

You might guess ten or twenty people lived there. As we walked along the trail in the snow that was made by dozens of footprints, I'd say there had to be closer to fifty or sixty people living here.

"Who did you call anyway?" I asked Brady as we stepped through the snow.

"I have a friend in the CIA. I told him where I was and how I got here. He said that Lee is someone they have been after for a long time." Brady explained. I wasn't surprised. Lee was involved in illegal dealings all over the world, but I was never able to prove it.

We reached a house on the other end of town. It was the last house before the white world that opened just beyond the hillside. I was never bothered by the cold. In fact, I liked the frigid air filling my lungs. It made me take notice of each breath.

The Chief's niece was just like I imagined her. She was sweet and had a welcoming smile. She'd begun making us some coffee when her husband asked us everything we saw while captured by Lee. I told what I saw, not leaving out any detail, then Brady told what he saw.

Brady's experience wasn't near as dangerous as mine, but it still nearly cost him his life. It seemed like only minutes had passed when the CIA agents came through the door. Brady stood to his feet and met only the agents with a firm handshake and a pat on the back.

I felt a sigh of relief wash over me. It was over. I felt a small sense of sadness because I knew this would be the last trip I would take. I wouldn't be able to continue the team without Seamore. I'd known all along that he was the reason I'd continued my father's research.

I wanted to keep my dad alive this way, but I just couldn't do this anymore. I didn't want to think about what I would do from here. I just wanted to go home.

Chapter 8

Stephanie's cookout brought all my friends to the house along with Brady and Josh's girlfriend Sarah, who I hadn't got the chance to meet yet.

Everyone was eating and having a great time. It had been one week since Brady and I returned from Greenland. Part of me wanted to feel like a failure because we came back empty handed. The other part of me was thankful that we had returned with our lives.

"So it's gone forever?" Josh asked me, right before taking a huge bite out of a hotdog.

"Yeah. I think I'm kind of glad. I've spent the last year and a half chasing that thing," I sighed.

"Yeah, but no one would blame you. A ruby that size and solid gold. It had to be worth millions," Josh grunted with his mouth half full. I knew he was right. The Viking ring could've taken care of us for a long time, but I couldn't let myself dwell on it.

I thought back over how I treated my father's work with the Alaskan Environmental research team. I loved what we did. What we stood for. Seamore didn't think I did a good enough job leading the team. I felt as if I'd lost my father all over again.

Could it be that I was afraid to focus on my father's work because I feared that I would let him down? Or do I really want to try something new?

I scanned the yard, taking in all the smiling faces. I couldn't remember the last time I was surrounded by so many friends and family members. It felt good.

"Thinking about Greenland?" asked Brady, appearing next to me. I nodded.

"You go on all these adventures around the world, but remember that this means more than all that," Brady advised, pointing his red solo cup to the group of people who would lay down their life for me. I may not have gotten my hands on the mountains of gold hidden in the hills of Northern Greenland, but I had to admit that I was still a pretty lucky guy.

The End

Authors Note

Thank you all for following along in this series. I loved this adventure and the characters. This story has a deep meaning for me.

I recently have had a part of my life come to a close, and it was bittersweet. I fought with everything I had to keep it alive for the sake of someone I loved, but I wasn't happy. I wanted something else.

Sometimes we need to take a step back and remember why we are doing what we are doing. Are we happy? Are we still in God's will? I hope this series inspired you. This will be the last book in this series………..for now.

Author Bio

Rebecca Hemlock is an Award-winning author and has written articles, books, and short stories for many years. She has worked as a freelance journalist for 4 years. She is currently a member of Sisters in Crime and American Christian Fiction Writers. Her books have also made it to the Amazon.com #1 bestseller list several times.

Rebecca has earned a degree in English and an Appalachian Studies certificate in Creative Writing. Her favorite times to write are early in the morning when the sun is coming up and at sunset. Rebecca lives in Eastern Kentucky with her husband and children.

Made in the USA
Columbia, SC
26 July 2023